The Three
Princesses

To:

carl

From:

By Lee Curniffe

ILLUSTRATED BY LEANNE ARMSTRONG

A Keivah and Daddy
bed time story

At the top of Mount Utopia, in a tall golden castle, lived a king and queen with their three princesses.

The eldest princess was called Kallisa but everyone just called her *Kallie*. Kallie had the biggest beautiful brown eyes you had ever seen.

The middle sister was called princess *Keivah*. She had the longest golden brown locks that went from her head down to her feet.

The youngest sister was called princess *Kiyanna*. She had soft, silky, golden brown skin that glowed in the sun

Princess Kallie

Princess Keivah

Princess Kiyanna

Duppy

The three princesses would always watch the children playing outside from the top of the castle window. The children played just outside the castle grounds but the princesses were never allowed outside.

A paper aeroplane flew straight through the castle window and landed perfectly in front of the three princesses.

It was an invitation to a party this Saturday night.

You are invited to our Summer Party!

Join us on Saturday

They asked their mother if they could go to the party but she said "Your father won't allow anyone to leave the castle until quarantine is over and COVID-19 has gone." So Kallie used her convincing eyes to gaze into her mother's eyes and hypnotise her.

It worked and they were allowed to go, but Kallie told her sisters that the spell will wear off by midnight, so they had to be back home **no later than 12:00am.**

Their father heard what was going on and tried to stop them from leaving the castle, so they had to creep through the dungeon doors to get out.

The princesses finally made it to the party.

It was the end of summer party and everyone was there. The Princesses could see everyone up close now and they thanked the boy who threw the paper aeroplane invitation through the window.

It was the best party ever and everyone was dancing and having lots of fun...

And then the clock struck 11:00pm!

Princess Kallie had already started to make her way home in an Uber cab.

Princess Kiyanna ran as fast as she could and made it back home at 11:45pm – just in time!

Princess Keivah had to climb up a tree to get away from a terrifying fire breathing dragon! So she called her mum on her iPhone and asked her to send some soldiers to capture the dragon.

Mother sent 12 soldiers to rescue princesses Keivah.

When the soldiers found princess Keivah and the dragon, they realised that the dragon didn't want to eat her. The dragon was lost and trying to find his way home – it was also only a baby dragon.

(Crowd says "Awwww!")

The soldiers got princess Keivah down out of the tree, and headed back to the castle. Suddenly, a huge dragon appeared out of nowhere – it was the baby dragon's mother.

The dragon used its giant claws to pick them all up. She flew them as fast as she could through the air.

Princess Keivah's hair was so long, it covered the mother dragon's eyes and she lost control!

Luckily, the princess and the soldiers landed in the castle! The only problem was, they landed on top of the king's breakfast table while he was still eating.

The king's breakfast ended up on his face and he was in a furious rage, until he realised that his lovely daughter had made it home in one piece.

The king laughed with joy.

Father

Mother

Soldiers

Mummy & baby dragon

Mother Tree

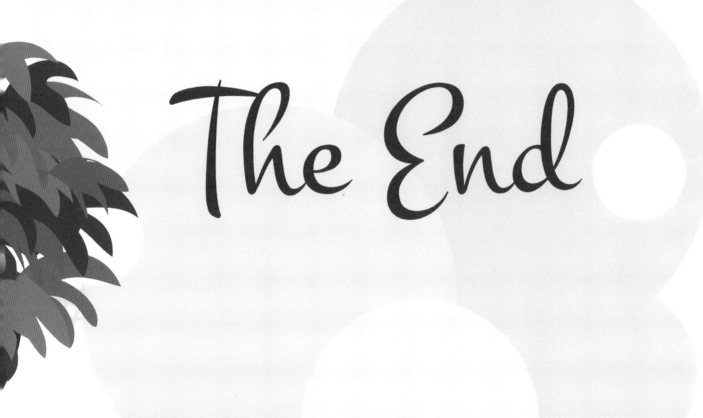

The End

To be continued likkle more…

Princess Keivah
loves to sing this song...

Oh Mister Sun, Sun,

Mister Golden Sun,

Please shine down on me

Oh Mister Sun, Sun,

Mister Golden Sun,

Hiding behind a tree...

These little children

Are asking you

To please come out

So we can play with you

Oh Mister Sun, Sun,

Mister Golden Sun,

Please shine down on me!

by Ananda Sen, Kids Songs,
Nursery Rhymes & Children's Stories

Printed in Great Britain
by Amazon